How to Make a Bedtime

MEG McKINLAY   illustrated by KAREN BLAIR

CANDLEWICK PRESS

When the sun's light is **fading**
and **night's** on the rise,
it's time to start **yawning**
your sleepy goodbyes.

Time for snuggling and snoozing
and **slumbering** now.
Time for making your **bedtime**,
and I'll show you how.

Oh, the first part is **easy**,
and here's how it goes . . .

sloshy-wash till you **sparkle**
from **tip-top** to **toes**.

Now you're rosily **warm**
and deliciously **dry**.
But you **can't** go to bed yet.
I think you know **why**.

Yes! You need some **pajamas**,
cloud-soft on your skin.
Once you're comfily buttoned,
you'll want to **climb** in . . .

But not yet! **Wait a minute!**
Don't tell me you're ready.
We **can't** call this a bedtime
until you find **Teddy!**

He's not on the **bookshelf**
or **under** the bed.
Oh, where is he hiding his
small **fluffy head**?

There it is, **pillow-peeking!**
So cuddle him tight,
burrow deep beneath **blankets**—
but don't say good night!

Though you're bathed and pajama-ed,
and **teddy-tucked**, too,
in the making of bedtime
there's still **more** to do.

Like a song for the **singing**
and listening as well—
a **lullaby**, whisper-fine,
clear as a bell.

Add a **huggily** hug
and a **smoochily** kiss,

and we're **surely** done now.
Shall we leave it like this?

Feel the night wrap around you
in **purpling sighs**,
as you're sleepily sinking . . .

Wait! Don't shut those eyes!

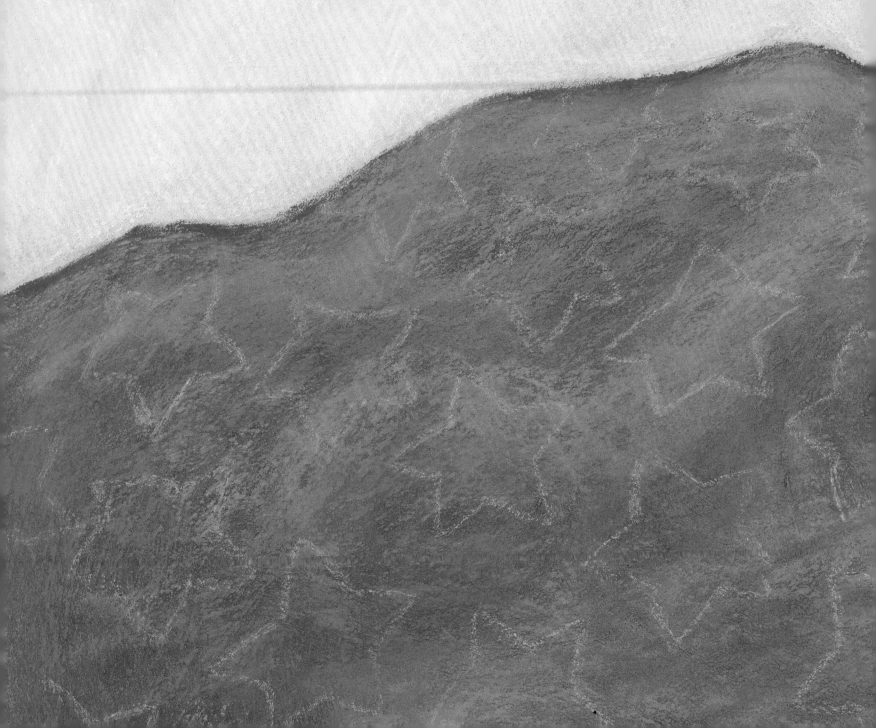

Oh, we're nearly there now
with our **cuddlesome** kissing,
our pajama-ly **calm**—
but there's still something **missing**.

Though you're feeling so
snuggily slumbery snory,
we can't call this a bedtime
until there's . . .

a story!

About
dragons
or
fairies

or
**rumbling
trucks,**

about
**tree-swinging
monkeys**

or
**quick-quacking
ducks.**

Or . . . a story like **this** one?
The one we just read!
About **bathtime** and **teddy**
and blankety **bed**.

When the **final** page turns,
when the telling is past,
when our story is **over**,
it's **bedtime** at last.

Now we've made us a **bedtime!**
We've done it, we two.
So there's just **one thing** left,
and it's all up to you.

It's to **snuggle down** drowsily,
dreamily, then
meet me back here **tomorrow**
and do it again.

First US edition 2025
First published by Walker Books Australia 2024

Library of Congress Catalog Card Number pending
ISBN 978-1-5362-3605-7

CCP 29 28 27 26 25 24
10 9 8 7 6 5 4 3 2 1

Printed in Shenzhen, Guangdong, China

This book was typeset in Bergamo Std.
The illustrations were done in acrylic paint, charcoal, and pastel.

Candlewick Press
99 Dover Street
Somerville, Massachusetts 02144

www.candlewick.com

To Hailey, for all the beautiful bedtimes to come
MM

For our Bedtime Bear, Karl
KB